Published by Disney Press, an imprint of Disney Book Group. No part of this book may be reproduced or transmitted in any form or by any means, electronic or mechanical, including photocopying, recording, or by any information storage and retrieval system, without written permission from the publisher. For information address Disney Press, 1101 Flower Street, Glendale, California 91201.

First Hardcover Edition, September 2015 10 9 8 7 6 5 4 3 2 1
ISBN 978-1-4847-1556-7
F383-2370-2-15170
Library of Congress Control Number: 2015935851

Printed in China

Visit www.disneybooks.com

Sofia the First

Sofia's First Christmas

Written by Laurie Israel and Rachel Ruderman
Illustrated by Grace Lee

Disney PRESS
Los Angeles • New York

It's a beautiful winter's day as Princess Sofia's coach lands beside Princess Vivian's snow-covered castle. "I'm so glad you're going to spend Christmas Eve with us!" Vivian says.

"Me too!" Sofia replies. "In Enchancia, our winter holiday is called Wassailia, so I've never celebrated Christmas before."

Vivian leads Sofia into the castle, where her parents, King Marcus and Queen Cecily, are decorating a great big Christmas tree. "Come help us trim the tree, girls!" Queen Cecily says.

Once the tree is trimmed, Vivian leads Sofia to where the Christmas stockings are hung. There's even a stocking with Sofia's name on it that has a little gift inside from Vivian!

Sofia takes a small present from her pocket. "My mom told me Christmas and Wassailia have one thing in common: that we give presents to the people we love. So I made this just for you."

Vivian leads Sofia to the gift wrapping room.
"Will you help me wrap the presents I got for my
family and friends?" asks Vivian.

Scissors snip, wrapping paper crinkles, and ribbons
fly through the air as the two girls wrap all the
presents.

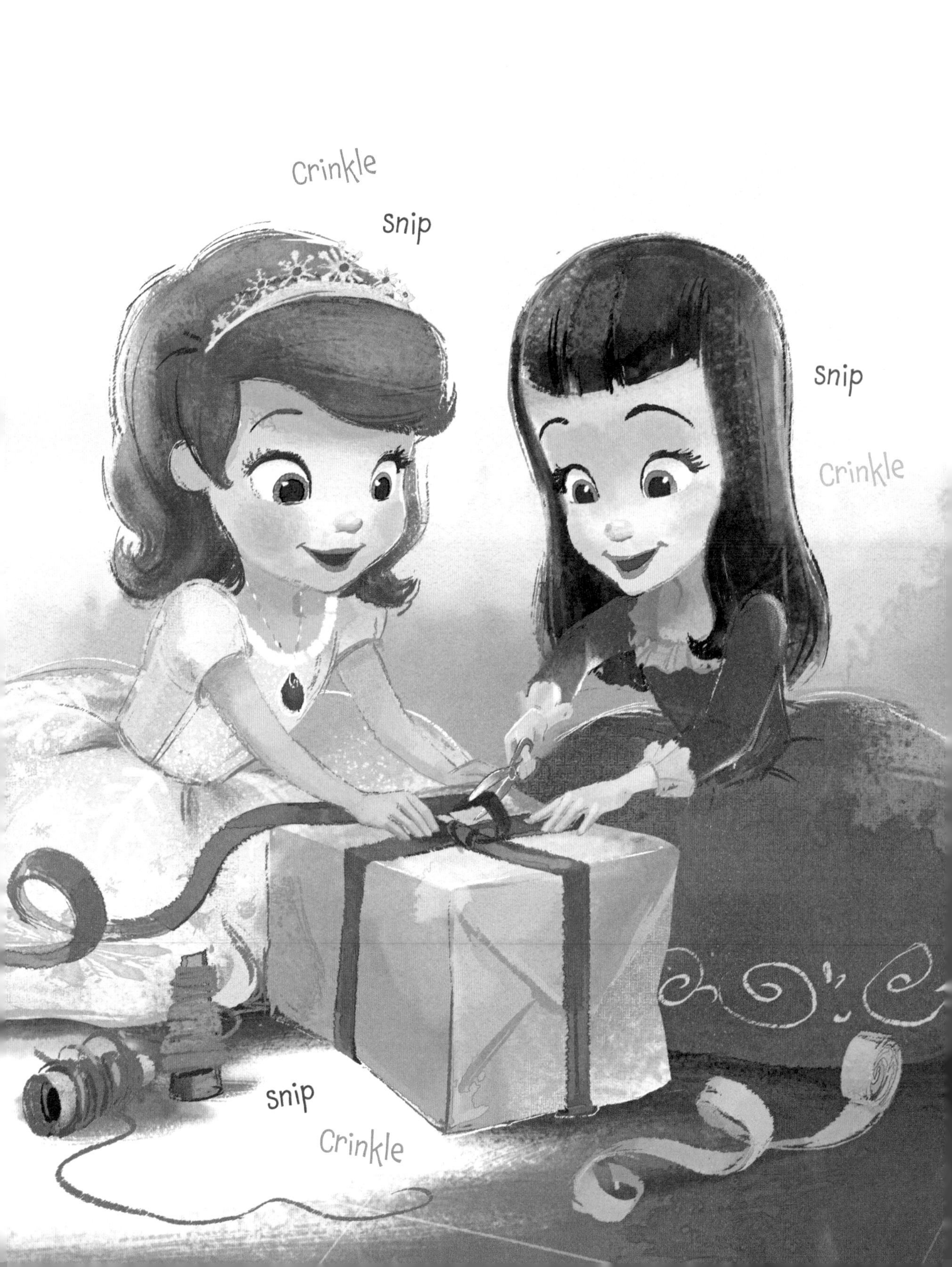
Crinkle
snip
snip
Crinkle
snip
Crinkle

"I'm having so much fun and it's not even
Christmas yet! What's next?" asks Sofia.
"Let's build a snowman!" Vivian says.
The girls find a hat, a scarf, and a few buttons.
"Just be home in time for Christmas Eve dinner,"
Vivian's mother calls.

Sofia and Vivian are putting the finishing touches on their snowman when, suddenly, his hat moves!

"Maybe it was the wind," Vivian suggests.

But then the hat moves again. Sofia lifts the hat to find her old friends Benngee and Button, two tiny elf-like creatures called wee sprites.

"It's so good to see you, Benngee and Button!" Sofia says. "Where's Brody?" The two wee sprites suddenly look sad.

"We haven't seen him for a while, and we're a little worried," Benngee tells them.

"We always spend Christmas Eve together, all three of us," Button adds.

"We'll help you find your friend," Sofia and Vivian both say.

"Where was the last place you saw Brody?" Sofia asks.
"We were swinging from these candy canes," Button answers.
"Then I jumped off, and Button jumped off. But Brody was
just . . . gone," says Benngee.
Sofia and Vivian search around the gazebo but have no luck.

The friends hear some pretty music. "It sounds like it's coming from my enchanted garden," Vivian says.

Button gets excited. "Brody loves playing instruments. Maybe he's the one making that music!"

Sofia and Vivian rush into the enchanted garden and find Herb, the hedgehog who lives there. Herb is conducting the garden's magical plants to play pretty holiday music.

Jingle!

Toot!

Toot!

Jingle!

Toot!

Toot!

Not here.

While Vivian and the sprites split up to look for Brody, Sofia talks to Herb.

"Welcome to my Christmas concert," Herb tells Sofia. She can understand him because her amulet lets her talk to animals.

"Have you seen our friend Brody?" she asks.

"Little guy? Loves to dance and shout 'hunga bunga'?" asks Herb.

"Yes!" Sofia tells him.

"He was here earlier," Herb says. "But I'm not sure where he went."

Not here.

Sofia points excitedly to the ground. "Look! Tiny footprints!"
"Let's follow them. Maybe they'll lead us to Brody," Vivian says.
Sofia thanks Herb for the concert, and they all hurry out of the
garden, following the tiny footprints.

The footprints lead to a clearing full of reindeer.
And not just any reindeer—these reindeer can fly!

SWOOOOOOSHHHHH!!!!!!

Benngee sighs. "They look awfully happy together,"
he says.

"Everyone is with the people they love," Button says,
"and we should be with Brody."

Sofia sighs. "We're right back where we started."
"And still no sign of Brody," Benngee says glumly.
"This will be the first Christmas Eve we've ever
spent without him," Button says.

Then Sofia hears someone calling out, *"Wheeee!"*
Vivian and the sprites follow Sofia to the hills behind Vivian's castle, where they see Brody riding toward them on a sleigh!
"Hunga bungaaaa!" Brody calls, then stops right in front of them.
"Brody! We've been looking for you all day," Benngee says.
"We were so worried!" Button adds.

"Gee, I'm sorry," Brody tells them. "I wanted your Christmas present to be a surprise." He shows them the tiny beautiful sleigh.

"You made this?" Benngee asks.

"For us?" Button adds.

"Uh-huh. I used wood I found in the forest near some flying reindeer and decorated it with flowers from the garden. Merry Christmas!" Brody says with a proud smile.

"Thank you," Button says. "We love it."
"But more than that, we're so glad we're all together
again," Benngee says.

Jingle!

Jingle!

"Sofia, we should head back to the castle. Christmas Eve dinner is starting soon," says Vivian.

"Do you have time for a sleigh ride?" asks Benngee.

"A quick one," Vivian says. "I'll get my toboggan from the castle."

Sofia asks Brody, "How did you learn to make a sleigh, anyway?"

"Some jolly guy in a red suit taught me!" Brody replies.

Later that night, the two girls open the gifts they made for each other. "I love this necklace! Thank you, Sofia," Vivian says.

"And thank you for the notebook, Vivian!" Sofia exclaims. "I can write all about the wonderful Christmas I spent with you and your family."

Just then, the wee sprites whiz past the castle window. "*Whee!*" Brody shouts out. . . .

"Hunga bunga
to all, and to all
a good night!"

The End